A Family for Old Mill Farm

For my nieces—all country girls at heart: Angie, Lisa R., Heather, Lisa C., Kelli, Katie, Joanna, Shannon, and Sunny
—S.C.

For David and Marie Philip, with love
—N.D.

Clarion Books
a Houghton Mifflin Company imprint
215 Park Avenue South, New York, NY 10003

The illustrations were executed in watercolor and digital media.
The text was set in 16-point Maiandra.

www.clarionbooks.com

Printed in Malaysia.

Library of Congress Cataloging-in-Publication Data

Crum, Shutta.
A family for Old Mill Farm / by Shutta Crum ; illustrated by Niki Daly.
p. cm.
Summary: When animals seeking new homes see Old Mill Farm, they know that it is just right, while human house-hunters, shown a variety of houses by their realtor, finally make clear what they are truly seeking and wind up at the farm as well.
ISBN-13: 978-0-618-42846-5
ISBN-10: 0-618-42846-1
[1. Dwellings—Fiction. 2. Animals—Fiction. 3. Real estate agents—Fiction. 4. Stories in rhyme.]
I. Daly, Niki, ill. II. Title.
PZ8.3.C88643Fam 2007
[E]—dc22
2006011336

TWP 10 9 8 7 6 5 4 3 2 1

A Family for Old Mill Farm

by Shutta Crum

Illustrated by Niki Daly

Clarion Books • New York

"I've got just what you want:
A really remarkable home!

"Here at Breezy Lake Lodge,
you can hear the seagulls cry
as waves wash up on shore
and boats go zipping by.
Make your home right here,
where the clouds just skim the sky."

"No, Breezy Lake Lodge
is not the home for us.

"Where do the tall trees grow?
Where do the songbirds fly?
Although we like the wind-tossed waves—
they're too splashy and too high.

"May we see another house, please?"

"At Old Mill Farm,
there are trees that touch the sky,
and they sway to and fro
with a song and a sigh.
Raise your babies here,
to a gentle lullaby.

"Raise your babies here,
Mama Finch, Papa Finch.
Be a family for Old Mill Farm."

"Perfect!"

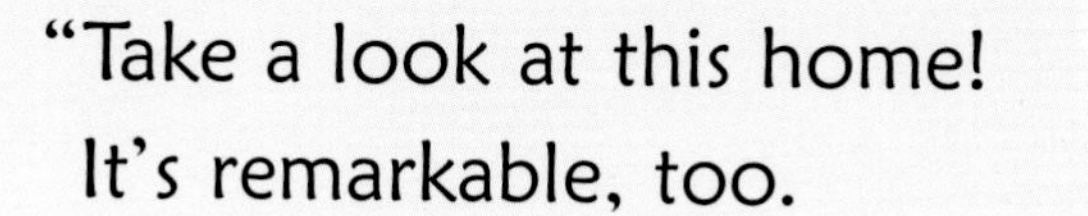

"Take a look at this home!
It's remarkable, too.

"Here at Dry River Ranch,
the breezes never blow,
and there's not one blade of grass
that you will have to mow.
Make your home right here,
where the prickly cacti grow."

“No, Dry River Ranch
is not the home for us.

“Where do the minnows flash?
Where does the water flow?
Although we like the landscape here—
it’s too sandy, don’t you know.

“May we see another house, please?”

"At Old Mill Farm,
beneath branches hanging low,
there's a shimmering pool
with a dragonfly show.
Raise your babies here,
where the water lilies grow.

"Raise your babies here,
Mama Duck, Papa Duck.
Be a family for Old Mill Farm."

“Perfect!”

"How about
this truly remarkable home?

"Here at Rocky Point Lighthouse,
all the sand is swept away,
and everything's scrubbed clean
by ocean tides each day.
Make your home right here,
where the beacon lights the bay."

"No, Rocky Point Lighthouse
is not the home for us.

"Where are the sunlit rooms?
Where can we dance and play?
Although we like the nice high view—
it's too stormy and too gray!

"May we see another house, please?"

"At Old Mill Farm,
there's a loft of tumbled hay
that is warmed by the sun
shining in throughout the day.
Raise your babies here,
where they can pounce and play.

"Raise your babies here,
Mama Cat, Papa Cat.
Be a family for Old Mill Farm."

"Perfect!"

"Well, here's *another* remarkable home.

"Here at Mountain Peak Perch,
where sunny skies abound
and clouds float far below,
the air is fresh, I've found.
Make your home right here,
far above the noisy town."

"No, Mountain Peak Perch
is not the home for us.

"Where can we take a walk?
Where is the level ground?
Although we like the endless sky—
it's too scary to look down!

"May we see another house, please?"

"At Old Mill Farm,
there's a gently sloping mound
where the sweetest grass grows
by a hollow in the ground.
Raise your babies here,
where there's room to hop around.

"Raise your babies here,
Mama Rabbit, Papa Rabbit.
Be a family for Old Mill Farm."

"Perfect!"

"*This* home's remarkable, too.

"Here at Briarwood Cabin,
there are lots of things to do:
take walks on hidden paths;
pick pails of berries, too.
Make your home right here,
where the roses bloom for you."

"No, Briarwood Cabin
is not the home for us.

"Where are the open fields?
Where is the distant view?
Although we like the clinging vines—
they're too thorny to squeeze through.

"May we see another house, please?"

"At Old Mill Farm,
under summer skies of blue,
there's a wide-open meadow
that is waiting just for you.
Raise your babies here,
where the grass is tipped with dew.

"Raise your babies here,
Mama Fox, Papa Fox.
Be a family for Old Mill Farm."

"Perfect!"

"One more remarkable home . . .

"Here at Prairie Place Park,
where the sky meets east and west,
you can wheel this trailer in
and be welcomed like a guest.
Make your home right here,
in this cozy mobile nest."

"No, Prairie Place Park
is not the home for us.

"Where are the shady rooms?
Where would our babies rest?
Although we're three, we'll soon be four—
in case you hadn't guessed.

"So, may we see another house, please?"

"At Old Mill Farm,
there's a wood lot facing west.
With a stream and deep shade,
it's a safe place to rest.
Raise your babies here,
in a dappled, hidden nest.

"Raise your babies here,
Mama Deer, Papa Deer.
Be a family for Old Mill Farm."

"Perfect!"

"This one is . . . well, there's this house, too.

"Here at Old Mill Farm,
there's room for quite a few.
The house just needs some paint . . .
a roof . . . a board or two.
Make your home right here,
with a view and, ah, lots to do!"

"Hmm! Old Mill Farm?
Is this the home for us?

*"We love the woods, the hills, the pond,
and the barn all tumbled with hay.
We love the stream, the sun, the shade,
and the meadow, where children can play.*

*"Yes, we want it. No other house will do.
Thank you! Thank you!"*

"Remarkable!"

"Perfect!"